W9-AZW-491

Happy 5[...] [...]!

Love, Kathy and Joe

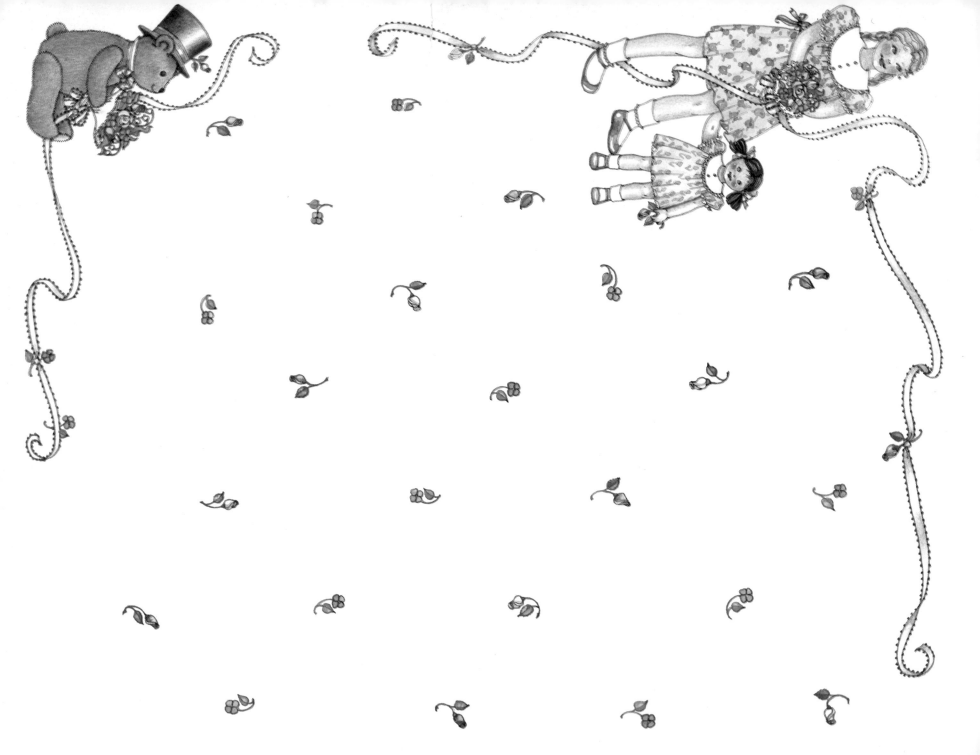

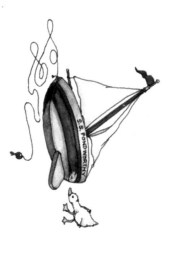

This book is dedicated to my grandparents,

Dorothy, for her imagination...

Harry, for his ingenuity...

Manya, for her strength of character...

And Willis...who was my sunshine.

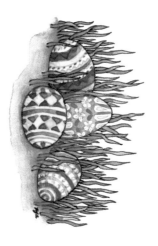

When Springtime Comes

by Ronnie Sellers

Illustrated by Peggy Jo Ackley

CAEDMON

New York

Art direction by Carlo DeLucia

Text copyright © 1984 by Ronnie Sellers
Illustrations copyright © 1984 by Peggy Jo Ackley

All rights reserved. No part of this publication may be
reproduced or utilized in any form or by any means, electronic
or mechanical, including photocopying, recording or by any
information storage or retrieval system, without permission
in writing from the Publisher. Inquiries should be addressed
to Caedmon, 1995 Broadway, New York, NY 10023.

Library of Congress Cataloging in Publication Data

Sellers, Ronnie, 1948-
    When springtime comes.

    Summary: A child imagines spring as a time for flowers,
Easter, picnics, kite flying, and many other things.
    [1. Spring—Fiction] I. Ackley, Peggy Jo, ill.
II. Title.
PZ7.S456994Wh   1984   [E]   83-23988
ISBN 0-89845-276-7
ISBN 0-89845-277-5 (library)

Published by Caedmon, New York
Printed in the U.S.A.   First Edition
10 9 8 7 6 5 4 3 2 1

hen springtime comes, I'll awaken one morning

To find that my room is all warm from the sun;

There will be robins outside of my window,
And I'll know for certain that spring has begun.

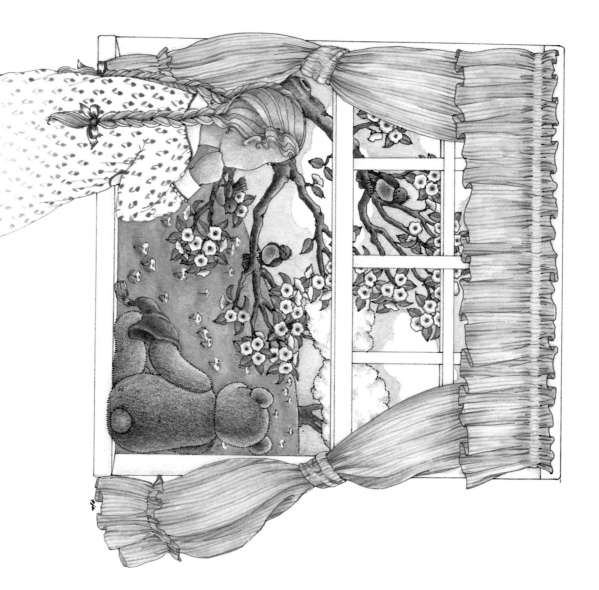

When spring arrives, it's a wonderful feeling;

Sweet-smelling fragrances perfume the air.

Baby birds hatch and the apple trees blossom,

And flowers begin to pop up everywhere.

When springtime comes, all my friends will come calling,
And we'll go together to play by the pond;

We'll have a picnic and launch our toy sailboats

And throw out some bread for the ducks and the swans.

Often, in springtime, the weather is breezy;
That's when I'll go fly a kite in the wind.

I'll let *my* kite soar up halfway to heaven—
And then I'll ask Daddy to help reel it in!

When springtime comes, I will help plant the garden
With lettuce, tomatoes, some carrots and peas.

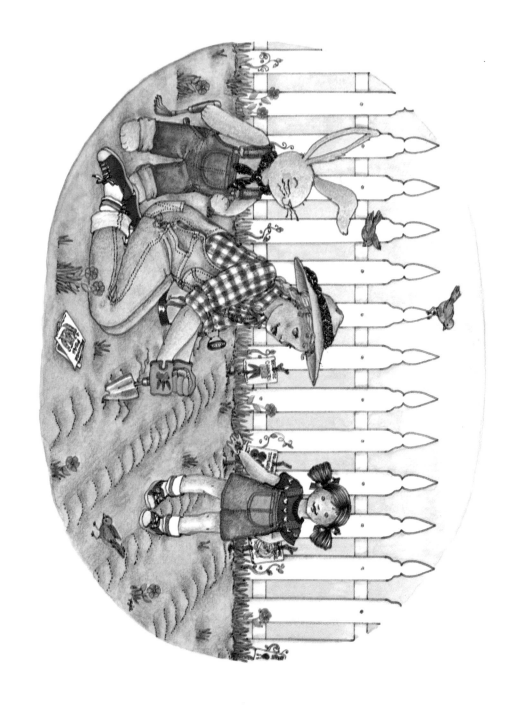

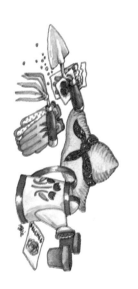

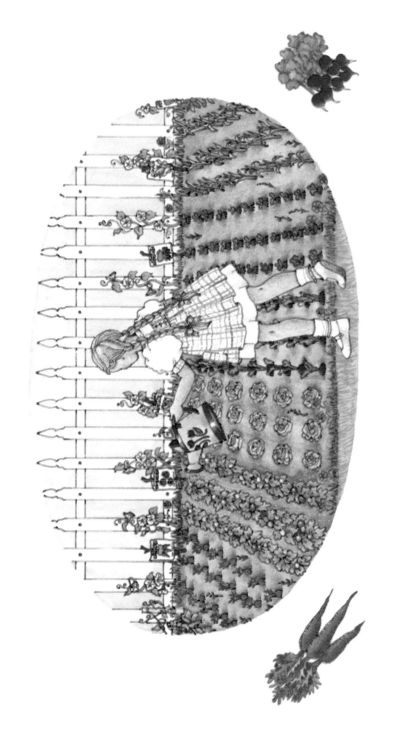

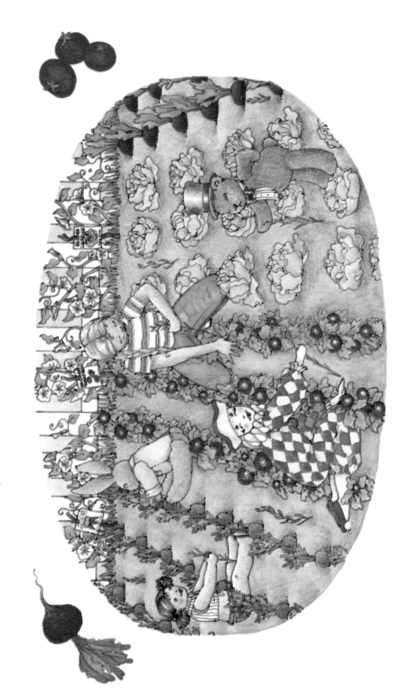

It will be my job to give them all water—
But everyone will have to help pull the weeds!

Sometimes, in April, there will be spring showers
To help grow the flowers that come up in May.

I'll wear my rain suit and big red galoshes
And look for some puddles in which I can play.

As Easter nears, I will do some spring shopping
To find a new bonnet, some shoes, and a dress.
It might take hours to find the right outfit,
'Cause I'll want to make sure that I look my best.

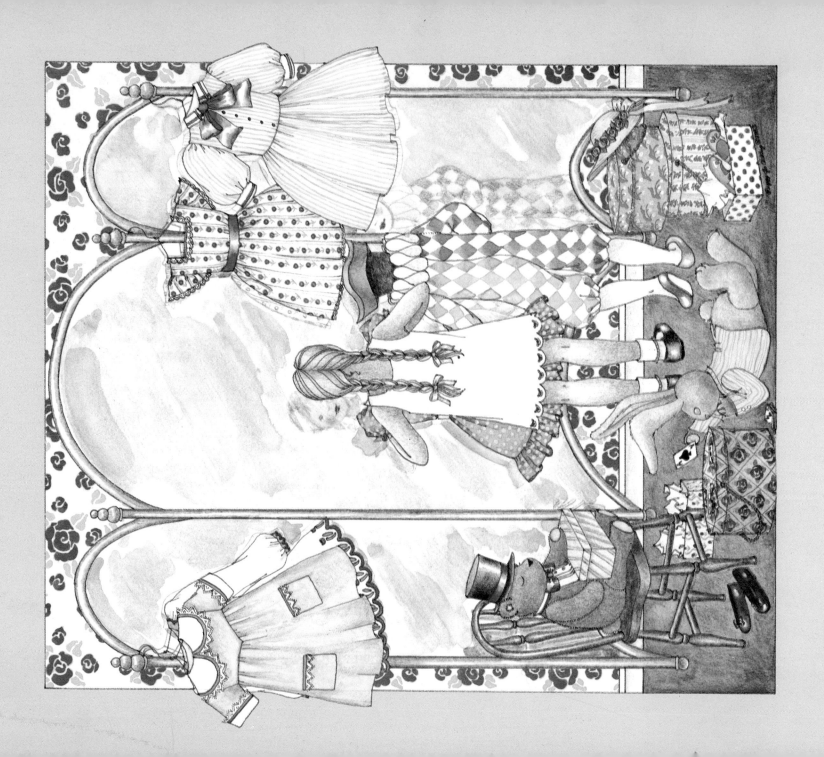

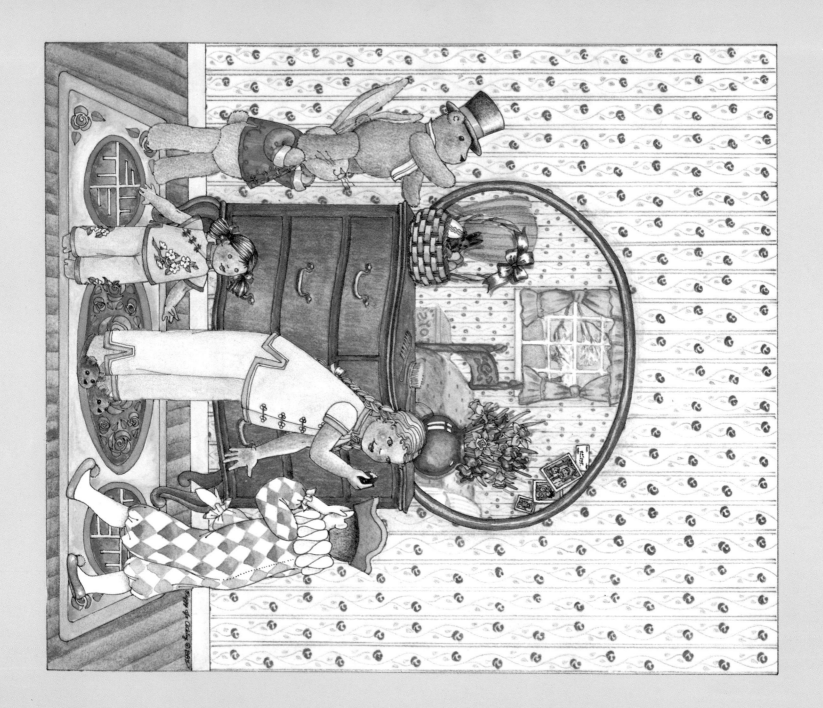

On Easter morning I'll look for a basket,
With dyed eggs and candies left 'specially for me.
I'll try to wait until later to eat them—
But no one will mind if I *taste* two or three!

Then I'll get dressed in my pretty new outfit
And go off to church with my family and friends;
We'll say our prayers and sing songs together,
And all will be happy it's Easter again.

Then, after church, we'll go out to the orchard
And look for the Easter eggs hidden inside;

I'll look behind every stone, bush, and tree trunk,

And maybe I'll win a nice Easter surprise!

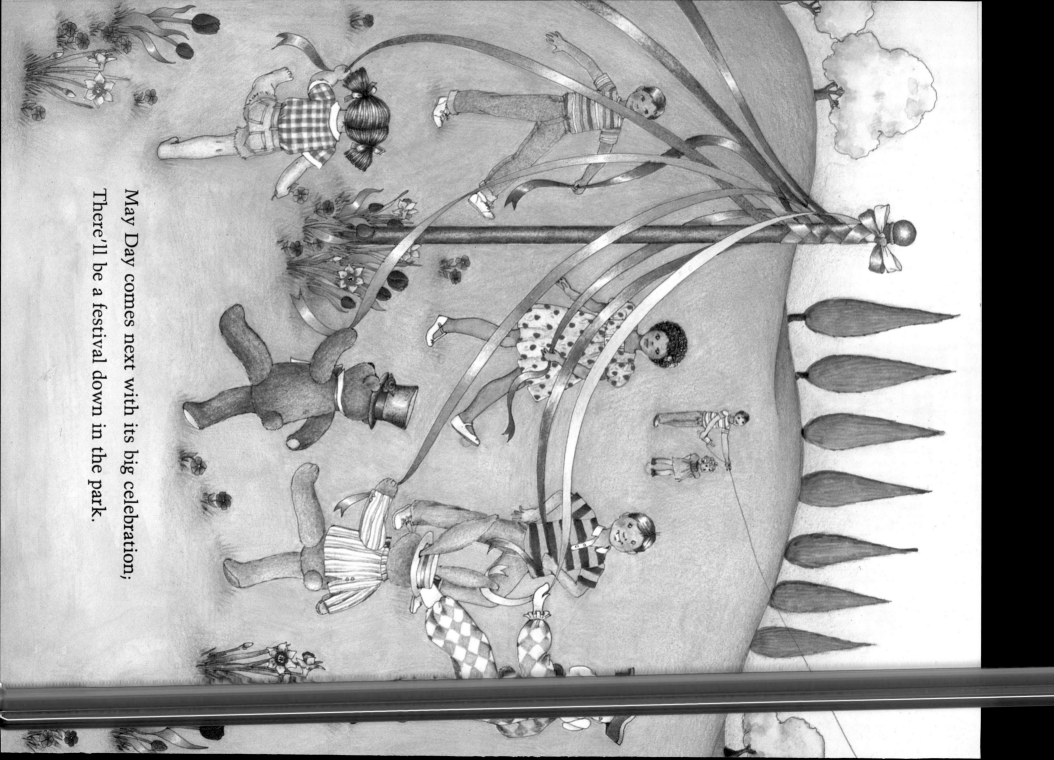

May Day comes next with its big celebration;
There'll be a festival down in the park.

We'll make a maypole and have some foot races
And ride on the ponies until it gets dark.

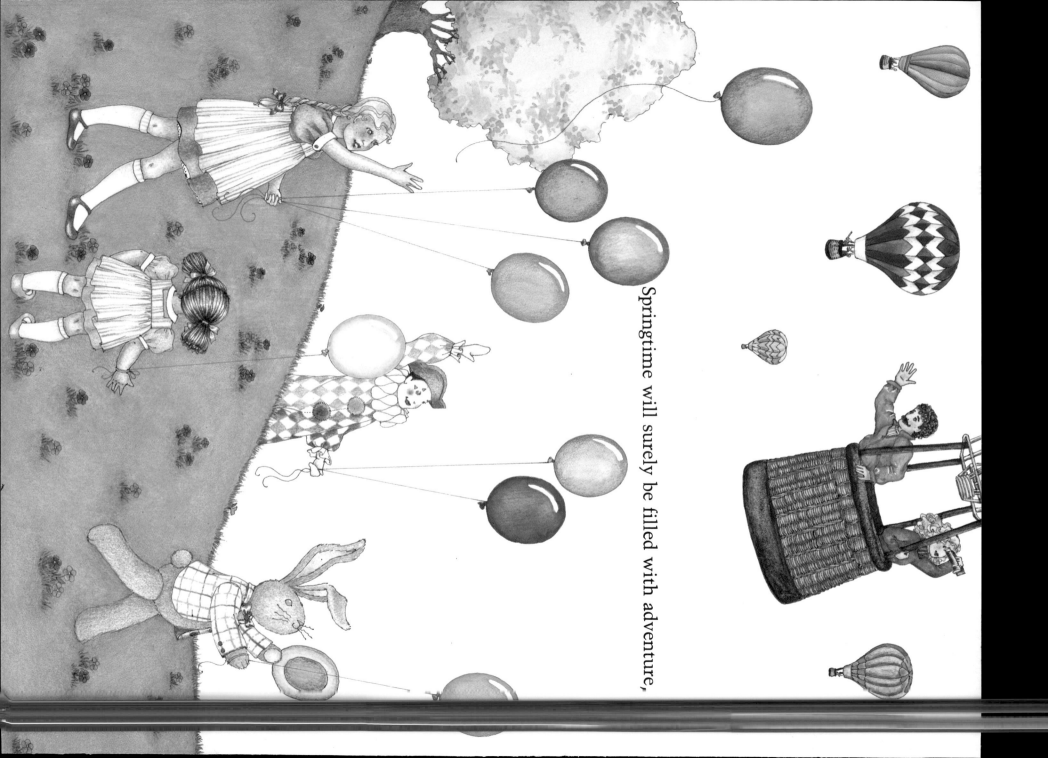

Springtime will surely be filled with adventure,

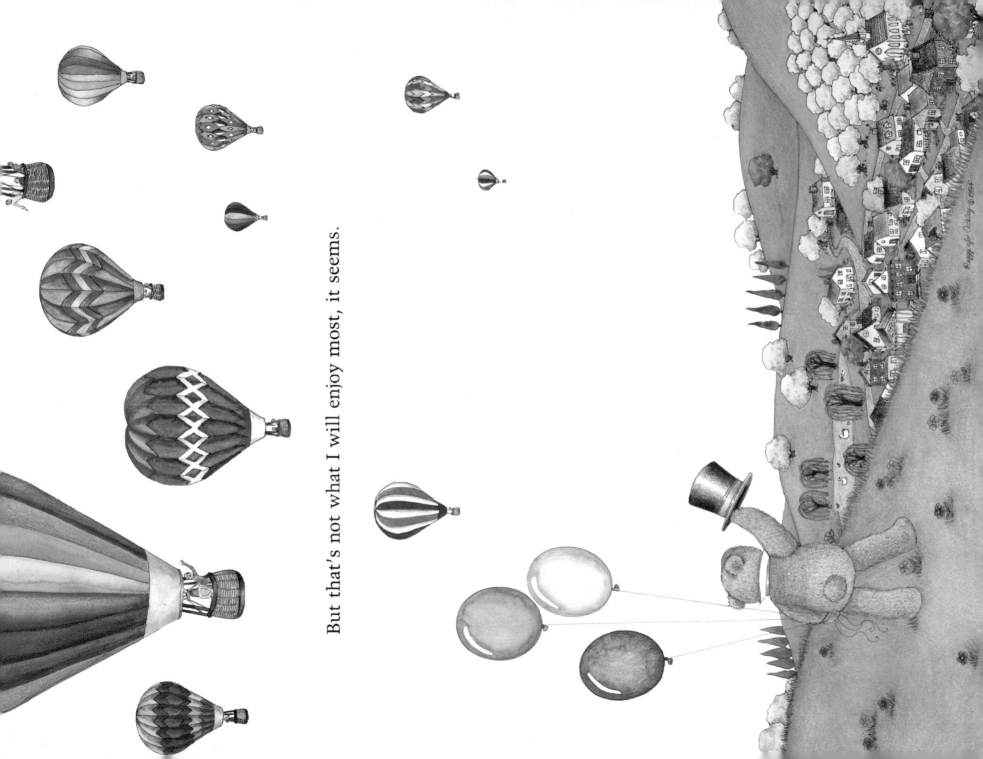

But that's not what I will enjoy most, it seems.

I think what I'll like to do best when it's springtime

Is lie in a field full of flowers . . .

and dream.